THE HEDGEHOG

Other Books by H.D.

THE HEDGEHOG

BY H.D.

INTRODUCTION BY PERDITA SCHAFFNER
WOODCUTS BY GEORGE PLANK

A NEW DIRECTIONS BOOK

Publisher's Note: *The Hedgehog* was privately printed in 1936 at the Curwen Press of London for the Brendin Company in an edition of three hundred copies for the friends of H.D.

Manufactured in the United States of America. New Directions Books are printed on acid-free paper; clothbound editions are Smyth sewn. First published clothbound in 1988. Published simultaneously in Canada by Penguin Books Canada Limited.

LIBRARY OF CONGRESS
Library of Congress Cataloging-in-Publication Data

H. D. (Hilda Doolittle), 1886–1961.
    The hedgehog / H.D. : woodcuts by George Plank.
        p. cm. (A New Directions Book)
    Summary: Living with her mother in Switzerland during the time of World War II, Madge moves from the concerns of childhood to the edge of the more adult woes of love and loss, separation and community.
    ISBN 0–8112–1069–3
    [1. Switzerland—Fiction.] I. Plank, George, ill. II. Title.
PZ7H1112He 1988
[Fic]—dc 19   88–3927
                                                                                    CIP
                                                                                    AC

New Directions Books are published for James Laughlin
by New Directions Publishing Corporation
80 Eighth Avenue, New York 10011

CONTENTS

INTRODUCTION
by Perdita Schaffner

"All books are about oneself," my mother used to say. She was referring to fiction. Poetry came from a different distillation. The novels hewed close to life, her life in full cry, characters disguised in name only; transcripts of direct experience.

Then, one day—I have no idea when it was—she decided to try something entirely different. It may have come to her in a flash, or gradually, as she was gazing out on the giant postcard view from her window. Whichever way, it wasn't easy. She was incapable of dashing things off. She envied those driven fiery geniuses who could stay up all night, working on until they burned out. Her inspiration would not be rushed. It evolved from painstaking thought and a lot of day dreaming, in the privacy of her room or out in the open air, strolling along the lakeside. There were false starts, stalled projects to be put aside, taken up later, and finished; all in good time and when the time was right. She scribbled early drafts in school exercise books, revised them on the typewriter, a huge rackety machine given to skewed margins and jumpy spacing, but then she did hurl herself at it with terrible velocity. She kept the typescripts in big folders, custom made in Florence—bound in heavy paper with floral designs, knotted with thick leather thongs. When she traveled, the "office" went along too. She set it up in hotel rooms, or the London apartment where she spent part of the year. Those were the days of surface travel, train compartments piled high with Madame's luggage, porters at every stop.

I was familiar with her habits and her work space. When I tiptoed in to say good morning she would be sharpening the long yellow pencils—Venus logo, worn-down eraser at the tip. I remember the texture of those folders, thick as wall paper; and the sheaves of erratic typing she wouldn't allow anyone to read. She was very protective about work in progress, feeling that any discussion would cause it to shatter like deep sea treasure suddenly exposed to light and air. Consequently I have no idea when *The Hedgehog* was written, nor how—steadily as an important project, or one she turned to intermittently for fun.

She revealed—casually, over the teacups—that she had a manuscript, a story, well not exactly a story, too long, not exactly a novel, too short. A little book for children set in Switzerland, no not really for children, but about a child, about me, well sort of.

Oh dear, would she ever stop thinking of me as a child? I was a full-fledged adult now at 14 or thereabouts. Those summer excursions to Alpine pastures were very sweet and wholesome, but kid stuff. I'd long since put Heidi behind me, exchanged her for the persona of a potential movie starlet. H.D. and Bryher were so cerebral, above such things as make-up and hairstyles. I set out to be flamboyant. I listened to jazz by the hour, spent my allowance on lipstick and eye shadow, fiddled with my hair. I was impossible.

Now, having raised teenagers of my own, I realize I was normal. She didn't offer to show me the manuscript; I didn't ask to see it. We left it at that.

Bryher had taken over a literary magazine, *Life and Letters Today*. Robert Herring, former film critic of the *Manchester Guardian,* was the editor; Dylan Thomas one of the early contributors. It was published under the aegis of Brendin, their own privately subsidized firm. From time to time they brought out attractive pamphlets—collections of essays, film criticism, poetry. They considered adding *The Hedgehog* to the list. A book for children, they agreed, should be illustrated. They already had their artist in mind, George, if he were willing, if he could spare the time.

George Plank, originally from Carlyle, Pennsylvania. He and H.D.

knew each other "when." He was part of her circle, along with Ezra Pound, William Carlos Williams, Marianne Moore. A cover for *Collier's* magazine—his first commercial break—was spotted by Conde Nast, who offered him a permanent assignment on *Vogue*. His individual style caught on. He was very successful, much as he despised high fashion chic and all the intrigues that came with it. His work being of the kind he could do anywhere, he took it to England, the country he loved most. He bought a cottage in Sussex, made it his studio and home, returning to the States for a couple of months each winter. He was an exceptionally well-balanced man, gregarious, with a wide circle of friends; and self-sufficient, content with his bachelor life, the garden, the kitchen. He was a superlative cook. Devoted to H.D. and Bryher, he was also, on quite another level, my friend. His calm philosophical advice helped me over many bumps. Tell it to George. We frequently lunched together, tête-à-tête. I spent weekends in his cottage, on my own. We corresponded. He wrote beautiful letters, responsive to joys and sorrows. So it was to the end of his long and happy life.

They all, between them—H.D., Bryher, George, Robert Herring and the Brendin Company—proceeded to put *The Hedgehog* together. It was published in 1936.

My adolescent revolt had calmed down by this time. Moreover, the book wasn't really about me. It was about Switzerland, a mother and daughter situation; the child's quest for a hedgehog; adventure, misadventure; safe return with the prickly prize in a cardboard box. A charming, deftly told tale, swift of pace, with George's delightful illustrations capturing every nuance. My opinion then, as I try to reconstruct it now, more than fifty years later.

Limited edition, 300 copies, collectors' items. I put mine away in a special safe place, and never saw it again. Carried off by some unscrupulous borrower, stolen, or most probably lost in the crates of innumerable house moves. I wonder what became of the other 297, and whether any were read by children.

After Bryher died her effects were shipped over to my house in Long Island, and there, in still another set of crates, I found two copies of *The Hedgehog*. Slightly warped and stained, pages pale beige rather than pristine white, yet in fair shape considering the passage of time, the sea change. Half a century, three thousand miles from the landlocked Swiss countryside to ocean shores.

I have now re-read it several times. Déjà vu? Only in dimmest memory. There is so much I'd forgotten, more which I hadn't fully understood. For all its directness H.D. has told a complex tale, filled with mystical allusions and poetry. She also makes a universal statement about loneliness, courage, communication—and the importance of sticking to a project and seeing it through, no matter how quixotic it may seem. A parable from another era. No jet trails in the sky, no television antennas on the chalet roofs, and the English shilling worth more than a Swiss franc. Superficial details of no importance whatsoever. As Bett tells her daughter, "Alpen-rose must be no year, but part of everything."

Bett is an American-born war widow, Madge consequently one of the Father-which-art-in-Heaven children of the world, a vast society of semi-orphans bonded by loss. Eschewing the English relatives' conventional standards, Bett has chosen to raise her child far away and free in a small Swiss village.

Madge, "a funny little independent individual," is oddly preoccupied with adders, both resentful and intrigued. Because of them she has to wear heavy boots in the meadow. Spotting a wiggly tail under a garden rock— a harmless grass snake or a large earthworm—she assures a visitor, Mrs. Hayes, that it is *only* an adder, possibly a whole nest of adders. The poor lady goes into hysterics, tea cup and hat askew, and leaves very quickly.

A neighbor, Mme. Beaupère, advises Madge to get a hedgehog. She should consult Dr. Blum, who runs a kind of nature preserve in his lakeside home. A *hérisson,* it was called in French, and what might that be? An animal the size of an elephant, a talisman, a bunch of medicinal herbs? She doesn't stop to find out. First things last. She tears off on her quest, impetuously taking a short cut down the cliffs. She gets stranded on the edge of a precipice, terrorized. Her pale André—the woodcutter's next to last son—rescues her, and after a sound scolding, sets her on the right path.

Dear avuncular Dr. Blum does indeed have a hedgehog, several in fact. The mother has just had babies.

Mission accomplished.

"All books are about oneself."

Bett is a magical mother. She has a lovely way with words, with myths. True. She is a maddening mother, overly concerned about dark woods, deep currents, snakes and boots. Also true.

As for Madge: she is the protagonist, the story is told through her eyes, her thoughts and language. But who is she? Bett's alter ego, junior grade, I venture to say. Me, in appearance and general concept. I was bumptious at that age, a bulldozer of a child, rampaging on in the here and now. Spiritual élan was up in my mother's sphere.

And, true again: the elided Bett-Madge has a keen sense of observation for scenery, for people on their daily rounds. Subsidiary characters are very much alive. She is quick to pick up the absurdities among some of them—the chauvinistic girl guides from English boarding schools, the tourists in their silly garb, Mrs. Hayes with her terrible old hat.

H.D.'s writing stands on its own. Yet I can't imagine this particular book without George's added vision, the wit and warmth of his illustrations. The very touching " Children of the World" circling their globe. The hilarity of Mrs. Hayes and her flying tea cup. Dr. Blum peering over a large tome, to pronounce: "A *hérisson* was used by the warriors of Mycenæ, who made caps of his rough skin. A *hérisson* was also used in the Athenian markets for the combing of wool; is that what you wanted?" And finally, that key figure, the hedgehog himself; the stance of his paws, the precise alignment of prickles—so real, ready to trot right off the page.

THE HEDGEHOG

ALPEN-ROSE

I

'My name is Madge,' said the little girl. '*Quoi*,' said Madame Beaupère, '*quoi donc?*' Which means, well what do you mean by trying to tell me that anything like that means what you seem to think it means. '*Madd, c'est pas un nom,*' and by that she meant, 'Madge isn't a name at all.'

'My name,' said the little girl, swinging two hob-nailed large little boots from the top of the woodshed above the vegetable garden at the back of Monsieur Beaupère's little shoe shop, 'is, I tell you, Madge.' Madame Beaupère and Madge always had this little dialogue, though Madame knew that Madge was Madge, and though Madge knew that Madame knew her name perfectly, they always went on in this way.

Madame said '*quoi donc*' again, and went on knitting solemnly. Madame Beaupère had a lot of knitting to do. She knitted in the summer, contrary to Madame and Mademoiselle Yvette, who spent the summer killing moths and stoning cherries for the odd sort of guests that always filled their house.

Madame and Mademoiselle Yvette treated their lodgers like visitors rather than like tourists, for the very same people came every summer at the very same time and remembered always to give Marie and the two Riboux orphans the very same tip. Most people give a franc; Madame Yvette's 'guests' tipped in English shillings, and Madame Yvette's Marie and the two Riboux orphans know that an English shilling with the picture of King George on it is much more than a franc. Madame Yvette's lodgers always gave the Riboux orphans and Marie each a shilling, which they took (to be changed) to Cook's in the main street of the big little town, down below their own little town, Leytaux, that perched above everywhere on a ledge of woodland. You get almost a franc and a half for an English shilling with a picture of King George on it. Madge knew that, even better than little Swiss Marie and the two very Swiss Riboux children. For Madge was, wasn't she, English?

Madge decided to be English some days. Other days she said

she was American. Bett, who was the mother of Madge, was American, but Madge's father had 'gone away' long ago (when Madge was just a year old) in that queer war. So Madge was both English and American. You would think she was French too, or Swiss, when you heard her speak; her funny little voice came from such a funny little 'foreign' sort of person when she said to Madame Beaupère, 'I came to see if Monsieur would take the nails out.'

Madame Beaupère went on knitting. She hardly stopped to glance at the little boots that Madge was swinging at her over the edge of the woodshed roof. Madame Beaupère shook her head over her knitting needles. She said, 'Madd. No. I think I would not do it.' Madame blocked the doorway, set there like some enormous great bush, Madge thought.

Madge, sitting on the woodshed, saw Madame from above, a bit of nose sticking out from under a sort of overhanging boulder of gray hair. There was a knot of hair on the top of the heavier, firmer bit of gray (that Madge called a boulder) with a round hole in the very middle just the right shape and size for a wren to make a nest in. Madame was round, her body bulged all ways.

Madge felt like a bird perched on the woodshed, peering down. Rows of very bright green new peas went straight in bright green lines toward the two curtains that were folded back and tied in the middle like doll-house window curtains. Madame Beaupère's feet looked like little flat dark blue felt cushions on the large brown strip of rug across the stones before the open doorway.

From the doorway, back of Madame Beaupère's low-backed broad low chair, Mew poked gray whiskers. Mew regarded Madge ironically.

'Mew looks at me as if I were a bad stray puppy or another kind of stray cat,' thought Madge, fretfully feeling great hobnails in her two heavy little rough boots. Madge suddenly was annoyed with everything. Madame was too fat and Mew was too impertinent. There was no fun stealing cherries from peaked ridiculous Mademoiselle Yvette this year, since Bett had told her most firmly just how it wasn't really much fun to take things from people who needed the things that you took. Bett was a dreadfully reasonable creature, and reasoned the fun out of so much pleasant mischief. Madge, perched on the roof, looking down at Madame Beaupère, thought suddenly, 'Now Madame Beaupère is the sort of doll-house person who should be one's mother.' Bett did spoil things.

Madge called her mother Bett because she hadn't any brothers and sisters, and Bett had short hair anyhow, and didn't look like the mothers of the Girl Guides who had come out from England at their school vacations. Bett wore a pull-on woolly most of the time, like Madge's pull-on woolly, only with longer arms, and Bett had the same kind of short hair that had to be brushed all the time to keep it out of your eyes. Bett was a very good friend, though she didn't seem like other people's mothers, and she did spoil things terribly. This whole afternoon, for instance, had been spoiled by Bett saying, 'You can't run bare-foot up in the upper garden, Madgelet. You must wear your thick shoes if you're doing gardening.'

Looking down at the fat comfortable knobs of Madame Beaupère's blue dress front, and the edge of the pattern on the blue and white linen apron that Madame wore (Madge knew) fastened by two tapes tied around the back under her arms, Madge was most resentful. 'Now Madame Beaupère is the sort of mother who would let you do things,' Madge thought, as she slid down the woodshed roof and landed neatly on the worn patch before the woodhouse door, most carefully not brushing the scarlet runner beans that wound round poles along the shed side. Madge could be trusted to respect other people's bean poles and their sweet-pea lattices (Madame Beaupère's sweet peas were trained across pine branches) and their rows of green peas and perky little radishes. Madge had her own garden. She knew all about taking care of gardens. That was the whole, whole trouble. Just why was Bett so fussy?

Madge sauntered toward Madame Beaupère, swinging her little too-short blue skirt. Her little too-short skirt showed incredibly grubby knees, incredibly scratched and incredibly valiant. Madge never paid any attention to her knees. If you begin to think about them, they defeat you. Madge had her funny little old philosophy, she knew so many little odd things. She was certain Bett was quite wrong this time. She approached Madame Beaupère perkily, perking up her really ridiculous little nose like one of her own most impertinent radishes. '*Madame, croyez,*' she said in her most grown-up French voice, '*ma mère m'a dit qu'il faut porter les souliers quand je fasse le jardin.*' Madge said that her mother made her wear shoes while she was gardening in such a funny unnatural affected little way that Madame dropped her knitting. 'Well, scallywag,' she said in her own language, 'and why should you not naturally obey your own dear mother?' Madge perceived that her grown-up manner had not quite worked. She tried another, more familiar, modelled on another pattern. 'Listen,' she said, this time slurring over her words like her big-boy friend, the woodcutter's second to the last son, André, 'I hate shoes. You know.' Madame did know. Though, as Monsieur Beaupère was a shoemaker by profession, she shrugged her fat blue shoulders non-committally. 'You know how it is. André and all the boys go, even in the Jamain forest if they want to, without boots. The vipers never bite you.'

VIPERS

2

'*Ça, c'est ça.*' Madame was now standing, half a shoulder pushed inside the little low door. Madame looked too wide for the little low back door of the low-roofed back of the house that at the front had quite an imposing entrance with a row of flat stones, and was Monsieur Beaupère's little boot shop. Madame looked like a doll that is just a size too large for that particular doll, house. Madge looked at Madame and back to the green peas that ran in green lines like green chalk lines drawn straight on brown paper. Madge had her box of crayon colours and her strips of dark brown paper, and paper not quite so dark brown, and she drew just such gardens often. Madame Beaupère's garden and Madame Beaupère's house and Madame Beaupère were just such draw-able sort of things as you look far to find, even in such a draw-able town as Madge's town, which was Madame Beaupère's town, which was the little French-Swiss town of Leytaux. Leytaux lay above a really large town, where lots of people came, running back and forth and up and down the hills for different things in different kinds of seasons. This was the summer season, a season which drew tall English ladies in wide old hats to Madame and Mademoiselle Yvette's. This was the time for the summer vacation sort of tourist, who was a very different sort of tourist from the winter tourist who came in bright-red mufflers and green pull-on woollys and enormous fur gloves. The tourists (winter and summer alike) were just as far away from Madge and her Englishness as were the Girl Guides. Madge was a funny little independent individual. She came back now to vipers.

'I tell you, Madame, André tells me, and Claus tells me, that never, never has any Leytaux boy ever been bitten by a bad snake.' Madame looked at Madge. Madame was sidling now further into the little back entrance to the little boot and shoe shop, and Madge sidled in unconsciously after. Madame became still larger inside the little hall-way. A clock in the corner, just the right size for the corner, clicked open its little clock door and let out a cuckoo. The cuckoo opened its cuckoo wood wings and opened its vermilion-painted cuckoo mouth and wheezed 'co-coo'. He stopped there, waiting. Madge said, 'I thought you told me last time that Belle was better.' (Belle was the cuckoo.) Madame did not condescend to answer Madge while Belle got over its first wheeze and achieved a full-fledged sort of little-bird-bark of a co-cooooo-oo. Madame did not trouble to answer Madge, but her fat right shoulder edged a suspicion of a shrug in the direction of the cuckoo. Belle then achieved a whole cuckoo, not stopping in the middle this time. Now Madame said triumphantly, 'She eeze bet-tair.'

Madame, it was apparent, had burst into English, so Madge, being a polite little Leytaux child, answered Madame in that language. 'You see, Madame Beaupère. It's perfectly ridiculous. There was just the tiniest tail of the snake. It might have been a grass snake. That old hag, Miss Hayes, screamed. Mamma was serving tea in the garden under the red umbrella. Of course, I thought it was funny, and I said, "Never mind, Miss Hayes, it is only an adder." Miss Hayes jumped a mile. She almost shook off the nasturtiums on her old hat. She always wears the same awful old hat with different bows and berries. Last year she had purple velvet, this year orange bows with nasturtiums. Last year she had velvet morning-glories with the velvet. Her hat made me laugh so that I added I thought there was a whole nest of adders, just to see her jump more. Mamma was very angry when Miss Hayes left in a hurry, and said, since I was so sure there were adders on the

upper slope, I shouldn't work in my garden without shoes.'
Madame listened intently. She peered forward and her shoulders
were drawn tight in her effort to understand. She had a pained
look and a cautious look as Madge proceeded. Madame wanted
awfully to have Madge think she understood her.

'O la, la,' ventured Madame, and then heaved a fat sigh. After
all, what was the use of trying to learn English? 'That eeze bet-
tair,' she said again, not knowing in the least what Madge had
been telling her, except that there was something about snakes.
'That eeze bet-tair'; then, before Madge could continue, she
burst into, 'la, la, vipers! You should have a hedgehog.'

HÉRISSON

3

Now Madame Beaupère said *hérisson*, which is the French and the Swiss-French for hedgehog. Madge, who understood most anybody's French, somehow for the moment couldn't remember just what was a *hérisson*. Some kind of heron, perhaps, she thought, and wondered what herons had to do with vipers. 'Vi-iipers,' as Madame called them, would not stay around where there was a *hérisson*, and she advised Madge to tell her mother to get a *hérisson* from old Doctor Blum, who used to keep a supply of them for all the villagers. Now old Doctor Blum, as Madge well knew, had the little villa with a statue of a boy holding a fish and another statue of a boy holding a dead bird which had a fountain basin for them to stand on, down on the lake drive. The lake drive was miles and miles away, or looked miles and miles away as you faced the down-drop of the rocks of the tiny mountain village Leytaux. One side of Leytaux was shoved tight up against the forest, tight and tight, so that there was no space of garden clearing between the little perched houses and the enormous great green forest branches. The other side of Leytaux was shoved almost over the edge of sheer cliff that fell almost to the lake that lay now, in the shimmer of the summer heat, far and blue and slightly misted over the edges with another gray-blue. Doctor Blum, as Madge well knew, lived down there, and Doctor Blum, as everybody knew, collected birds and had cages of birds from time to time which he studied carefully. He was a very kind and careful sort of person, and let the birds fly away when he had studied the marks on feathers and how they changed the feathers. Doctor Blum was German-Swiss, but as Madame Beaupère said, 'la la, his grandmother, old Madeleine Reboux, was one of us, so that he comes from Berne is no great matter.' It was a long, long time ago that old Doctor Blum had left Berne, but everybody still called him Doctor Berne Blum to distinguish him from the other Blums who came from Maux further up the valley. People and names meant so much in Leytaux.

Now Madge thanked Madame Beaupère very nicely. She hoped

if she thanked Madame Beaupère very nicely that Madame
Beaupère might sort of let, as they say in English, the cat out of
the bag. Madge was reminded of that English metaphorical (as
Bett called it) expression by the sort of ironical twist of Mew's gray
whiskers. Mew was looking at Madge, and Madge realized that
she had stayed a very long time just talking about nothing, for the
cuckoo, who came out every quarter hour, was almost ready to
pop out again and co-coo in that mawkish rusty way he had of
doing. Somehow Madge felt her visit hadn't been altogether a
success, for Madame hadn't suggested her leaving her shoes there
as Madge had thought she would do, and having Monsieur Beaupère take the nails out later. Madge had thought that out most
carefully, thinking that when her mother said, 'But I *said*, darling,
you must wear your boots working in your garden,' *she* could say,
'But you see, mamma, I had to leave them at Monsieur Beaupère's
to have the nails out.' But Madame Beaupère hadn't kept the
boots, nor had she even by any shrug of shoulder or heave of
round blue bosom intimated that she sympathized with Madge
about her mother. Madame had, in fact, not sympathized in any
way, and there stood Madge with the great heavy little boots and
no Monsieur Beaupère in sight, and just this vague hint about
some kind of heron. 'Are they, she was going to ask, 'expensive?'
but was afraid Madame would realize she didn't know what a
hérisson was. It might be something people *give* you, like dried
mint or lavender. It might be some sort of herb or thing like you

have for moths. It may be a sort of thing like moth ball that perhaps old Doctor Blum would call snake ball, or some medicinal herb and not a living creature. 'Ah,' said Madge, knowingly, 'but yes, the very thing, a hedgehog.'

She said hedgehog in French, not knowing what it meant, and left Madame Beaupère knitting in the sunlight.

BIG LITTLE BOOTS

4

Madge's boots were heavy over her shoulder. Her shoulder was
half bare and very brown where her little thin blouse was pulled
half off. Half of the shoulder was very, very brown, the other bit
showing where the thin blouse pulled quite away was quite
another colour, so that Madge looked like two Madges—a very
brown Swiss Madge and a white clean little English or American
one. Most of the white English or American part of Madge was
hidden; the brown Swiss part was lean, very long, and arms very
thin but very strong, and shoulder and throat and out-pointed

determined little chin. The eyes of Madge were very, very blue. They looked out blue as only one flower in the world is blue, and that is the wild gentian. Now gentians are a very Swiss flower, so the eyes of Madge, in spite of everything, seemed Swiss eyes, too. Madge was a mountain goat, clambering bare-footed down the very, very steep side of the Leytaux hill that leads straight to the water. The steep side of the hill was a very Swiss side of the hill. No English Girl Guide, and no casual English or American tourist ever went there. Madge went quite carelessly like a bird or a mountain goat or wild sheep. Yet Madge went very carefully like a bird or a mountain goat or a wild sheep. Nothing worried her, not the sky, too far above; nor the lake, an inverted sky, too far below; or the barbs of prickly gorse or wild berry bushes. Nothing worried Madge. She was a wild little part of everything. One thing worried her. 'These hateful great boots. I was so sure that Madame Beaupère would have kept them.'

Madge didn't always calculate quite straight. Now something had alienated Madame Beaupère's sympathy. Was it the way she had spoken of her mother? 'O pooh,' said Madge, just out to everything, 'I can't be expected to put up with Bett's irritations.' Things that Madge's mother worried over, Madge thought, were so peculiar. Imagine being worried about Madge alone in the forest. The forest never hurt, nor the water. The lake never hurt you, but Bett would worry and worry about what she called cross-currents. It is true that the River Rhône ran into their lake, and the river, running into one side of the great lake (like a little sea) and out the other side, created funny whirlpools and little currents. But nothing, Madge was sure, could hurt you in the water, nothing could hurt you in the air or in the rocks. The only things that hurt were things like odd Girl Guides and hateful mothers who made you wear great heavy boots because there was or wasn't a poisonous serpent in your garden.

'Who-eee.' A voice up above Madge made Madge pause a moment, one foot fitted in a boulder, the other carefully planted on a space of dried grass that was the least berry-prickly of any she could find. Madge, standing with one foot very firm and half-curled round the boulder, and the other half-firm for fear of prickles, but placed square and carefully, looked up. Above her head the sky rose blue and blue, more blue now that she was half down the cliff side, as the rocks at her shoulder shut off half the fall of sunlight. A cloud was nosing its way up over the edge of the rock wall like the nose of a very white and very woolly big sheep. The blinding silver across the white cloud a little dazed her. Madge stood perfectly still, letting her upper foot settle firm in spite of prickles. The very slightest little bout of dizziness came over her. Dizziness on hill-paths was a new sensation. She clutched a little wildly at the upper bushes. Her hands laid hold of prickles. She tried to think naturally, wishing that voice had not jolted her out of her very safe descent. Madge found that it's better never to stop and think in the middle of a path that goes up the side of a hill or down the side of a hill like a snail-track on a house wall. The Leytaux hill seemed steeper than she had thought. Was it, perhaps, the dazzling silver light that caught that white cloud? The cloud seemed lowering nearer down to crush her.

ECHO

5

'Who-eee.' The voice came on again, high and low at the same
time. It was a voice within a voice, and that was, Madge knew, a
thing we call an echo. Now Madge loved these funny things called
echoes, and had often made Bett tell her the story of the boy who
was turned into a flower and the girl he loved called Echo. When
Bett told that story, Bett was the most lovely sort of mother.
Suddenly, a little dizzy and just a little frightened, all crouched
down under the prickly bushes, Madge thought differently of Bett.
There wasn't any Girl Guide or any girl at any of the little

Swiss-English or Swiss-American schools along the lake edge, or any girl anywhere, that had a mother like her Bett. Now Bett would tuck you up in bed and tell you such, such stories. The stories Bett told you were so beautiful that you certainly would have to cry if Bett weren't there watching and saying, 'Now you do understand, don't you?' Bett made Madge understand that the stories weren't just stories, but that there was something in them like the light in the lamp that isn't the lamp. Bett would say to Madge, when she was a very little girl, 'Now what is the lamp side of the story and what is the light side of the story?' so Madge could see very easily (when she was a very little girl) that the very beautiful stories Bett told her, that were real stories, had double sorts of meanings. One of those stories was the story of the boy called Narcissus who turned into a flower called narcissus because he loved his own lovely face so much. And that story always came back to Madge when she climbed far and far up toward the snow edges of the mountains in late spring to come back with green narcissus buds for Bett. Everybody climbed far and far up the hills for narcissus buds and white narcissus flowers just as later they climbed for the lovely blossoms of the Alpen-rose. Alpen-rose and gentians and early narcissus were all part of the woods, and all part (Bett said) of people's hearts in Switzerland. That is why Bett loved Switzerland and wanted Madge to love it. Bett said, 'Other people made wicked wars, but here people waited in their hills.' Bett wanted to forget a wicked war, and that is why she stayed here out of England, out of America, with Madge.

Tucked precariously into the ledge now, Madge had a little bout of tenderness. Uncle Harry was always coming out from England and saying to Bett, 'Now the child is growing up a perfect little savage.' And Bett always said to Uncle Harry, 'I would rather she grew up barefooted and on a daily crust here in the freedom and beauty of these hills, Harry, than have her provincialized and sterilized as you are doing with your wretched children.' Uncle Harry and Bett always laughed then, but Madge knew, for all the extravagance of her words, that Bett was very serious. Uncle Harry always pinched her cheeks and asked Madge if she knew her a, b, c yet, and if she had forgotten English. Madge politely let her cheeks be pinched, and made up the sort of baby-answer that she thought would please Uncle Harry, but she knew in her heart that Uncle Harry was what Bett called a hypocrite and an old fraud. 'Harry considers it patriotic to have his children speak French like *Punch* cartoon jokes of the year 1880.'

Bett had said to Madge, 'You must be no year at all, Alpen-rose, but part of everything.'

WILD BIRD

6

Now being part of everything is all very well when you're tucked up in bed watching the lights from the upper row of Leytaux chalets shine in your window, knowing that that light is the Riboux', that that light is Madame and Mademoiselle Yvette's, that that light is the strange 'guests' light up on the upper pathway. Little lights coming, going, great lights making one solid sheet of silver on a bedroom wall; there was no room in the world better for watching moonlight than was Bett's room. Watching the moonlight creep up like a veil, just waiting for the moment when it will spill over the sharp edge of the mountain, is one thing. Safe in bed is one thing. Being part of everything, safe in her own bed, or in Bett's bed, is one thing. Being part of everything out of doors after having had nasty thoughts about Bett, and after being decidedly snubbed by Madame Beaupère, is another. Madge clung to the very prickly bushes. There were the tiniest little shell shapes of flowers just out, the real little shell shapes of wild roses. These Bett called wild roses, briar roses or pasture roses. The Alpen-rose was different. But when Madge saw the little roses she remembered Alpen-rose, and how Bett called her Alpen-rose and said, 'Alpen-rose must be no year, but part of everything.' And Madge wished she hadn't (in her thoughts) quarrelled so violently with Bett and that Madame Beaupère had been kinder.

Madge blamed the whole thing on the shoes really, for if she hadn't gone up on the upper road to get Monsieur Beaupère to take the nails out of her shoes (which he hadn't taken) she wouldn't now be clinging, part of sky, part of lake, part of rocks, and very much part of everything, to the side of a cliff which has only the barest excuse of a snail-track of a path straight up among its boulders. All the small stones had slipped down long since, ages and ages since, before even Hannibal crossed the Alps (these Alps), before even Napoleon marched right straight through their valley (this valley) on his way to Italy. Long and long and long ago, as long ago, Madge thought, as the beginning of the first narcissus on their hills, the little stones had slipped down. Madge saw now that she

was the tiniest littlest part of everything, or, as Madge felt, clinging there really frightened for the first time in her funny little life,
she was the tiniest littlest part of nothing.

'Who-eee' came down nearer, it sounded huge and lowering
like the silver cloud turned thunder-black. Great thunderstorms
would break suddenly in their hollow of lake and sky, and suddenly Madge saw the rightness of Bett in being frightened sometimes. 'Who-eee' was like a thunder cloud, and Madge tried to
hold on to something that would bring her comfort. Bett said, in
those lamp-and-light Greek stories, that the thunder was the voice
of Zeus, and Zeus in those lamp-and-light Greek stories was the
father of everyone, so Bett said he was like the other God our
Father which art in Heaven, only the Greek light-in-lamps people
called him by another name. Thunder, if it frightened you, *did*
frighten you. Some people it frightened, some people didn't mind
it. That was like the voice of God. Poets and prophets had talked
with the voice of God on mountains. Madge was suddenly shocked
and frightened, thinking, maybe, the voice of God was going to
speak to her right here now on the Leytaux cliff side.

Now Madge had always envied the little boy Samuel and the
Greek light-in-lamps people when God spoke to them. Bett said
He certainly did speak, but somehow it was so very frightening
to be taken unprepared this way. 'Now please, please,' Madge
pressed her little tousled forehead against the prickly bushes, 'let
it be a lovely message, let it be a nice voice.' Madge prayed, very

frightened and very serious, into the wild rose bushes. 'Please, God in Heaven which art a part of everything, don't let Bett be angry with me; I didn't mean (in my thoughts) to be impertinent; please forgive me for having begun to act out a sort of half story-telling story about the nails in my boots (which didn't work anyway), and forgive us our trespasses as we forgive them which art in Heaven.' When she had finished this wild little prayer, she looked up. Above her head the cloud was the same, only a little less frighteningly silver, and below her feet the lake was the same, with the same little blurr-rrr of heat-haze at the edges. The little wild roses were like little rose-pink shells, and there was a wild bird high and high, turning and turning, like a wild hawk. 'Oh, there he is again,' thought Madge, really frightened this time after her wholesome little terror and her repentance, 'there is God again. Bett says He often turned into an eagle.'

FACE TO FACE

7

Madge scrambled to her feet. Well, she would meet God face to face, like the Greek boy does in the statue that Bett has. Bett had a statue of a small figure; she called it a Tanagra, as Tanagra is a tiny, tiny town in Greece (or was a tiny, tiny town in Greece) where they made these little statues that people prize now more than bags of gold and countless bags of silver. Madge had learned that there are some things that you really can't buy with great quantities of money, and that is why she and Bett felt so very rich living here alone in mountains, and that is why Bett always got fretful after Uncle Harry's visits and always consulted with Madge and said, 'Madgelet, perhaps I *am* wrong.' And Madge always flung her arms around Bett and said, 'No, no, Bett, we don't, don't want the money,' for it seemed there was a lot of money put away somewhere that depended on something, trustees or wards in chanceries or something like that, and in order really to get bags of this odd money, Bett and Madge (for some odd reason) would have to live in England. And Uncle Harry would come storming out about every twice or three or four times a year and say, 'Things get more and more awkward. You and the child should really live in England.'

Now 'England is one of the most beautiful islands in the whole world,' Bett used to say to Madge, 'and it is the lovely island that your father came from.' Now there was no argument when Bett said 'your father'. Not having a father, 'your father' said that way was just the same as 'our Father which art in Heaven', and made one feel rather swallow-y. There were so many, many children, Bett said, who had that kind of 'Father who art in Heaven' for a father, and such children, Bett said, were (must be) just a tiny, tiny bit different from other children. Now there was a great army of children all over the world—French children and German children and Serbian children and Turkish children and American children and Armenian children and Russian children. And all, all of these children, though they might never know one another, were all sort of odd little brothers and sisters (Bett said) and they must never, never hate each other, and they must never hate each other's countries, because every one of them had a sort of 'Father which art in Heaven' for a father, and they must feel differently about wars and about soldiers killing each other than other children. 'Each one of you children wears a bright crown,' Bett said, and that is why poor little Madge quarrelled with the Girl Guides. Now the Girl Guides are very nice sort of girls, and some of them very serious sort of girls, but they said, quite solemnly, that England should, and must, fight its enemies, and Madge said, 'England has no enemies but its own hearts,' which was an odd, frightening little thing to have said from nowhere, and though she didn't quite know what it meant she had had to stick to it, because children who have a 'Father which art in Heaven' for a father always are (Bett said) the littlest wee bit frightening.

WELTGEIST

8

Now, here is where Madge had a little bout of reconciliation with everything, for the Girl Guides (for some odd reason) were her special abomination, and she had to admit to herself, stranded there with no visible path now anywhere between heaven and earth, that Bett had probably been right when she had said: 'Madgelet. You are high up, like when you have inspirations, and low down, like when you steal raspberries and cherries from people who really need the little money they get from selling them in the market. Now the Girl Guides maybe don't have what you and I call inspiration, like *England has no enemies but its own hearts* (or France or Germany or America or Russia has no enemies but its own hearts), but they have, perhaps, a little more of something than has Madgelet.' When Madge asked what that was, Bett had answered, 'Well, just common or garden common sense, Madgelet,' and though Madge hated to think of the Girl Guides having anything that she hadn't, she had to admit (stranded between heaven and earth with prickles making regular gashes in her taut little bare arms) that perhaps the Girl Guides had points sometimes. The Girl Guides weren't *guides*, that was what Madge had quarrelled over, but then how could they be? Bett had pointed out: most of them were English schoolgirls and didn't really, really live in Switzerland, like Madge did. There was something, Bett said, that you got from living in a country, and from loving a country as she and Madge loved Switzerland. The *Weltgeist* sort of thing of that country gives itself, or might give itself to you. And it wasn't the fault of the visitors and the tourists and the Girl Guides and all the various schoolgirls in and about Leytaux, if they hadn't just what Madge had. Madge had something in her manner of finding her way about on the wildest hill-path, in her funny little way of speaking, that was 'native'.

Now, however, that 'native' thing just left her. Madge was quivering with cold terror, though the sun beat and beat down on her and there were hot little beads dripping off her forehead and running down her cheeks like tears almost. Tears of terror, they might almost have been called, for this *Weltgeist* seemed to have left Madge or, for some presumption, to have punished her. *Weltgeist* is a German word which Bett explained, for Germans have odd thoughts that sometimes no other people have, and their thoughts are sometimes so rare and so odd that there is no translation for them. One of these lovely thoughts or ideas was of a sort of Geist or spirit who ruled the world: a sort of person like the old, old Greek god that Madge read about, a light-in-lamp Greek god who was called Pan. *Weltgeist* was a sort of Pan, a god of terror and of woods, who belonged to everybody, and that Greek word stays the same too, since the Greeks have such lovely thoughts and such different thoughts that no words were ever found to translate them afterwards. Pan in Greek means everything, or everywhere, and the God who was a god of every-one, of all, all the wild things, was called Pan. *Weltgeist* and Pan were very much alike, and, shivering and trembling, clutching at the berry bushes, Madge cried, 'O *Weltgeist,* O Pan, O Our-Father-which-art, please somebody come to help me.'

The voice that had frightened Madge came nearer and she closed her eyes, hearing trampling and rushing through the bushes. Madge, with her eyes closed, wondered which god would find her: *Weltgeist,* whom she saw as a sort of Erlking (another sort of spirit, who stole a little boy in a song), or Pan, who, of course, she knew had shaggy legs and goat heels and a tail and goat horns, for there were lots of old Greek statues and copies of the Greek statues in books; or Father-which-art, who was the most difficult to visualise but who is there like Pan, part of everything all the time. When Madge opened her eyes she thought it must be Pan who answered her.

ANDRÉ

9

'Who-eee' kept on speaking out of a face that was so close above her own that, with the sun shining back of it, it looked very like the great blocks of rough stone people used to use for Pan statues. 'Who-eee', said again, very close and very mockingly, and very, very scornfully, close above the bushes, right against the sun, came to Madge mocking and jeering and not at all (somehow) frightening; though it was all odd and full of terror, it must be (she thought) the answer to her *Weltgeist*, Pan, Father-which-art sort of little mixed prayer. Someone, anyhow, had answered. It wasn't

certainly a voice like that which answered Samuel, so it couldn't
be Our-Father-which-art. It wasn't a voice like the voice in the
Erlking, which Madge connected in her mind with rivers and
streams and the mist above rivers and streams. Bett would play
that song for Madge often in the dark, and that song was connected with the beautiful word in Madge's thoughts that was the
word for which there is no English translation, which means a
sort of spirit everywhere, especially in streams and forests and on
the tops of mountains and all along the ledges of rocks where the
gentians and yellow violets grow and who is called *Weltgeist*.
Weltgeist, Madge thought, was part of the solid sheet of moonlight that lay on her wall, and that lay, she was certain, nowhere
so beautifully as on Bett's bedroom wall and that was jagged at
the edges by the distant rim of jagged pine trees that were black
against the moonlight in summer, and that in winter, spiked up
like single icicles turned the other way round, white with snow
and hoarfrost. *Weltgeist* went with trees and with rivers, and with
mist above river, but this was sun, and sun and mockery and
forests too, but a different kind of forests. This was forests with
sun and sun and, she was certain, little brown moles burrowing
into dark earth. This was moss turned a little brown at the edges
on the hot slopes after the streams have dried up, and this was the
dried stream-bed of summer slopes and the first brown leaves that
break off in midsummer because it is so hot. This voice and this
mockery was a shadow of a black, tall tree, a pine tree gone black

against sunlight, and it was the smell of the Riboux' orchard apples where they lie in little piles against the stones that is the rough way the Riboux' father (before they were orphans) had laid the orchard wall. This voice was the voice that ran and ran and ran and had no shoes on. Madge clutched the hateful shoes and suddenly remembered everything. Now she was just Madge, an ordinary, rather frightened, defiant little girl staring up at André.

André, the second to the last of the long row of huge boys who were the woodcutter's row of great boys and who were almost too big now (except André) to go to school, looked down at Madge. 'Madd,' he said, just as Madame Beaupère had said it such a little while (which seemed such a long while) since, 'you are one big fool.' André, the second to the last of the row of woodcutter's boys, said this, of course, in his language, which is the French language, but as André spoke it sounded another sort of language altogether. Madge could speak French carefully like all the people down below in the big little town, and she could speak French like the Mademoiselle taught it to the girls who came out from England and who came all the way from America to learn French, and she could speak it like Madame and Monsieur Beaupère, and she could speak it like André. She loved best what she called André-French, and looking up now she knew that André-French was the sort of French the Greek god Pan would speak if he spoke French and not Greek. The Greek god Pan must have spoken a funny kind of Greek, just as André spoke a funny

kind of French. The French André spoke was full of funny little
bu-rrrs as if, wandering in his own high woods and wandering
under and about his own berry bushes, burrs had stuck to André
all over, not only to his rough patched trouser knees, rough,
too-short sleeves, the back of the black mat of black hair, the
collar to the sort of half-leather sort of jacket that he wore sometimes with an apron, but to André's tongue as well. 'You are,'
said the woodcutter's second to last André, 'one great big fool of a
stupid idiot. Nobody ever comes down this side-path.'

Of course, there was one answer to that, and Madge made it:
'*You* come, André.' She was now quite comfortable, had let go
hanging on to the bushes, had dropped onto the little shelf of dried
grass where André dropped beside her.

ONE OF US

10

Of course, everyone knows in Leytaux that everyone is as good as everybody else. People who kept bees and cleared forests laughed at people who came out from Paris, who came out from London, and slid down slopes (where narcissus blooms in late spring) on bob-sleighs, but nobody ever let anyone from Paris or anyone from London know that they were laughing. In Leytaux you have a certain sort of laughter that hides behind your cheek-bones and that never comes out till long, long afterwards. Of course, Madge, because she spoke everybody's kind of French to everybody, was a little let into the secrets of what *fou* English did and what *fou français* did (who came from big, huge, rather dreadful cities, not *françaises* of the mountains), and what dreadful foolishness it was to open windows or to shut windows and to wear two pairs of stockings under huge boots when one pair or none would do much better. Madge was not a *fou* anything, she was just Madd, a rather naughty little girl who had a way, Madame Beaupère said, of saying the most *unnatural* things for a little girl born so far away as London with an American for a mother. Madame Beaupère said that Madd knew more about cuckoos in and out of clocks even than Françoise Riboux, who had collected eggs for old Doctor Blum all the years since Doctor Blum had begun that long book which he never finished. Even Madame Beaupère treated Madge like 'one of us', and it was disconcerting to see that sort of smile under cheek-bones flickering in and out under André's eyelids somewhere. The smile of André flicked and disappeared very much like that little black snake tail that had made a little whip shape under the peony bush in bud and that had flicked then out toward the row of half-grown heliotrope that needed watering. The little snake, Madge knew, was part of all things, part of the forest of all things that has Pan for its guardian. André sitting there now, saying just nothing to her, looked like a smallish Pan person, someone who knew everything, who was everywhere at all times.

'Well, André, you needn't look at me that way.' 'I tell you, I thought *you* had more sense.' 'More sense than what, Andrè?' 'It is only fools of *anglais*, fools of city French, fools of new Americans just off boat at Havre or Marseilles or Genoa who let themselves be caught up this way.' 'Caught up, André?' 'It is only fools, you know, who let themselves slide off the edge of mountains and come to an ugly splash below, just above Monsieur Blum's cottage on the lake-side.' 'André——' 'You would look pretty, wouldn't you, all smashed?'

André was a little serious now, and his face was white under all the very-Pan brown. 'André——' 'Who told you you could cut down the Leytaux cliffs? Nobody ever does it. I thought even the fooliest female *anglaise* would know that.' 'I do know—I did know——' 'But you—you—forgot, maybe?'

'Well,' said Madge, snuggled now close against the bushes, 'of course nobody saw me come down this way.' 'I saw you,' said André, and suddenly it seemed to Madge that André must see everything. 'You saw?' 'I saw you the whole time. I was up above, chopping toward Jamain. I saw a hawk swirling, and I always know when a hawk swirls that way, there may be a young sheep or one of Riboux' kids got loose. I saw him swirl, but it was only bad English meat that he was after.' 'Oh, André!' 'Children sometimes have been snatched up, babies (you can imagine what idiots) right off the floor or out of the garden by an eagle.' Now all this sounded oddly somehow quite familiar. 'You mean'— Madge could not remember the name of the person; then she did remember—'that boy who got caught away by Zeus. His name was Ganymede.'

Now André hadn't much use at the moment for Ganymede. He had clutched Madge under the arms, and half lifting, half jerking, half pulling, he had almost flung her out and out among rocks and boulders across bushes that scratched and slashed, up and out, then down and then across. André pulled and pushed and kept on saying: 'Fool, Madd. Don't for anything look down there.' Madge (when she did look) saw a lake blurred at the blue edges, a little house set just below among trees (lilac bushes and chestnut trees, she remembered), a tiny white flick of white that might be a sail or the white sunlight on a swan wing, the blurr of mist again, and . . . 'André, what cold water!'

ERLKING

II

The sound of water was the sound of the music that Bett made in the dark when she played *Erlking*. Erlking was a great mist-white creature of wood and water who stole away a little boy and Madge thought all at once that Erlking would have stolen her away (maybe he was in that white cloud) if it hadn't been for André. Now, dreams are all very well, and thoughts that come from nowhere that are a sort of inspiration, but there are other things that matter very, very much, especially for little girls who play by the sea or who take long walks in mountains. There is a kind of wood-lore or wood-love that drags people into the heart of woods, but there must be a kind of love to balance it that is just natural love, the sort of love that made André rush down the dangerous cliff after a little foreign girl who had been very naughty. There was a love that ought to have made Madge a little reasonable, the love of Madge for Bett, who, after all, although she had short hair and wore the same sort of pull-on woolly jumper, was really Madge's mother. Erlking was the thing that got hold of you and made you suddenly frightened, and Pan was the thing that got hold of you and made you wild and made you rush up hills and along river-beds all alone, crying and swishing at the bushes for sheer joy. But all this joy is no use if it leads you into danger, and all this joy turns a wicked thing (like some sprite or gnome or pixy) if it makes you hurt other people. Now, Madge had this sudden swirl of thoughts because of André saying, '*This time I tell your mother.*'

Now, many many times André had said, 'Now *this* time I tell your mother.' André had said that when Madge had been caught all alone among the lake reeds looking for the swan nest, and André, who had been fishing that summer afternoon, found her and pulled her out of the rushes and put her in the end of his boat and said, 'Now *this* time I tell your mother.' The fish nets had tangled about Madge's tired little scratched ankles, and the little lake fish in the bottom of the boat (she remembered) had flopped funny little lake-fish fins, and made flop-flop noises against the dried boards until she had baled out water from the lake in the old pail that André kept there and had made a little pool of lake water in the bottom of the flat boat. All her thoughts of the lake and the reeds, and the swan nest and the way the swan had darted out with great white wings, were linked up somehow with André. André was the swish of little lake waves and the cold days when the water came up quite high, like real sea-waves, and the swirl of gulls and the vermilion-red beaks of the gulls as they dart through the lake mist in winter toward the bread crusts and little odds and ends of tiny fish that Madge and other Leytaux children throw, sometimes even from their own windows, out toward the swirling gray birds. André was, it was evident, a sort of little Pan, knowing everything that had to do with woods, knowing so many things that Madge did not know. Of course, Madge knew lots of things that André did not know. For instance:

'This water flowing down here from the highest part of the hills, André, is a white nymph or sort of goddess. She is white. She is the colour of elderberry bushes, and she is the colour of the wild mountain ash in flower. This stream, André, has a real life. It was once a girl called—called . . .' Madge could not think of the name of the girl. 'Sometimes these girls are called Naiads, sometimes Oreads. The Oreads are the real mountain girls that live furtherest up the hill.'

André rested an elbow on the grass and on the little shelf of grass and moss and listened to Madge. 'The god Pan loved one of these especial girls who had a life in everything who was called Echo. She is the only girl of all the girls who will really answer you. Call her, André, not now, because it's closed in here like a green tunnel and the stream is rushing, rushing, making noises like the *Erlking* music. Some day, up on the hill alone, call this girl. She is the only one of all the girls who will answer. Call her Echo, Echo, and she will answer Echo. Or sometimes just O, O, O, starting from this hill going on to the next hill, all O, O, O, just the same O, getting thin and far and far and thin like the sound of water. Echo melts into the hill, into the water. Now she is a real person. Some of the light-in-lamp people you look for and never find. Echo is easy to find, and the boy Narcissus. The boy Narcissus is the white flowers on the slopes in late spring. He is so white that he looks like a ghost or a spirit. His breath is the breath of the narcissus, and when spring comes he rises from the black earth to tell us that there is a life after this life for everyone. Echo is the answer of our own hearts, like the singing in a sea-shell. You have never seen the sea, André. Some day, when I grow up, I am going to get a house by the sea. You must come and watch the waves with me and Bett, come in, go out. You must get real sea-fish in the deep sea-water.'

Now Madge knew perfectly well what effect all this would have on André. It was not the first time that she had struck that stubborn little goat expression across the black forehead of the woodcutter's second to the last André. The thing that made

André say, 'Now *this* time I will tell your mother', stuck out of the forehead of André, obstinate like the horns of a hill-goat, very like the horns of the god Pan. Madge saying 'Echo' like that, and telling her water stories, was hanging white flowers about the throat of André. André was a sort of goat-god sitting there, and all the sound of the water was in the voice of Madge when she kept saying, 'Now you won't . . . you *won't* tell mother?'

GENTIAN-BLUE

12

Now André wasn't rashly going to promise anything. He knew Madge and how Madge could wheedle and coax and tease and get almost anything she wanted from almost anybody. Madge had only to open gentian-blue eyes and blink eyelids that were not quite so burnt, and that when they rested a moment (in the blink) quiet over the gentian-blue eyes, were almost as white as that part of the shoulder of Madge that was always having a thin little blouse jerked up across it by Madame Beaupère or by other people's mothers. Madge had only to do this, to do that, and she could get anything she wanted. It wasn't quite fair, of course, but as Madge was not quite 'one of us', and yet, in a way, so very, very different from the strangers and the tourists and the usual foreigners, Madge got everything both ways. Madge, André thought, got everything all ways, so he wasn't going to give right in to Madge, straight at the beginning, as he knew very well that he would have to give in at the end, anyway.

'Well, anyway—what were you doing down this hill? Nobody ever comes here, not ever here by the Jamain river, as it is cold glacial water, and sometimes even the goats get lost here by the stream that flows from below earth and then suddenly, just at the top of the Jamain road, finds its way into Father Boudrey's hay-field.' Madge knew that the Jamain stream (or, as André called it, the Jamain river) had odd living ways with it, darting like a white bird with long white bird-of-paradise or white peacock-tail feathers, here, there, now spraying across rocks, now creeping, all in little spread feathers of streamlets (like a white peacock in the grass) across the Jamain meadows and right through Father Boudrey's hayfield. The hay was long grass really, thick with wild flowers, goldenglow that is a kind of enormous buttercup, like a golden button, blue, blue cornflowers, the bluest of blue forget-me-nots, the blue of violets that are always just a little different blue from anything, and little purple orchids. Madge had tried to make a crayon drawing of the Jamain meadow, and it came out only splotches of yellow and dark blue, and violet blue and different splotches of green everywhere. Now, that is really how the Jamain meadow did look, but somehow, when one put it down on the brown-for-crayons drawing paper, it just looked rather silly. Everything can be made into something else, but nobody could ever draw, Madge was certain, that meadow. Now she remembered the meadow and her funny botched drawing and how she had tried to put a cloud in the corner as it came over the edge of the small pines by the coppice, but it all looked very flat and very, very (for such a big girl) silly. Madge knew all about this stream and all about the rocks far above where it started, and all about the fields it flowed through, though she had never, it is quite true, seen it from just here, spurting down out of the rock, rushing through a sort of green tunnel, breaking like icicles (so cold and so pure) to rush (she knew) just past old Doctor Blum's front door where it again disappeared and went its own way, further than anyone could find, into the blue lake water. It is true she had foolishly got almost caught, just this once, on the precipice, and André had been scolding her, but André, she was sure, knew no more, not half as much about this very stream as she did.

Madge a little resented André not giving in to her at the beginning, as Madge thought, 'He has to give in to me at the end, so he might as well do it now and get it over'. André thought differently, so he glowered at Madge as he drew a long, very green, wet grass blade through his big white teeth. The teeth of André were too big for his boy mouth, though you could see that when André grew up he would fit his own teeth beautifully. Madge, too, had teeth that were square and fitted rather huge in her small mouth. Inspired by André, she too drew a long stem of grass through her square, big little teeth. The water was ice cold as she dipped her hand in, to draw the grass out full and long and cold by its deep roots.

'No. I think I will tell your mother. You had no right to be there.' André repeated this very solemnly. 'What, anyhow, did you want, sliding straight to perdition down the wrong way? There *is* the little path that leads right where you wanted to get, anyhow. Where *did* you want to get, anyhow?'

'I? Oh,' said Madge, 'I was going to old Monsieur Doctor Blum's to get a—to get a——' Now Madge suddenly couldn't quite remember the new, strange word. 'It was for snakes,' she went on, seeing André watch her fumbling with her story. 'We had an adder in our garden.'

A WAY OF LAUGHING

13

'Oh, vipers,' said André, vipers being no more to him than brown moles, than gray- and brown-speckled squirrels (speckled like a bird egg with little wood-leaf speckles), than lizards who are very near relations anyway to wood snakes. 'Oh, vipers,' said André in a funny little voice, as much as to say, 'You, Madge, what a female creature you are to think of vipers.' And Madge, seeing that little perked-up sneer on André's brown face, cried: 'Oh, it wasn't *me*, André, I love them, and anyhow maybe it really wasn't. It was that old Miss Hayes who made me angry coming and interrupting my own tea with mamma. Then, you see, I was so angry I made her jump saying there was an adder. Maybe a nest of adders.' André stood now with a little pulling of straps and settling of belt lines where he had got pulled about falling and sliding down the hillside. 'La, la,' he said, very like Madame Beaupère, 'it is quite true. Yes, she should have a hedgehog.' Now André said hedgehog in French again, and Madge waited, still wondering what it could mean. 'But it's not, you see, André, for old Miss Hayes—though'—this occurred suddenly—'we *might* take some to her.' 'Some?' said André. '*Quoi donc?*' rather puzzled. 'I mean,' said Madge suddenly, seeing that she might be discovered, 'that—it——'

'Yes,' André agreed. 'We might', he continued, 'take that—it to the old lady, but wouldn't the old lady', he asked, 'be just as much frightened by that—it *hérisson* as by the vipers?' Now Madge was much worse off than ever. That—it had done her no good. 'Oh, well,' she hazarded, not wanting to commit herself to anything, 'I don't know. It depends, doesn't it'—she had an inspiration—'how big that—it is this time.'

'How big?' André looked astonished. 'My dear Madd, do you have *hérisson* then as big as—as elephants in England?' André slapped his legs as he had seen the second to the top of the row of woodcutter's boys do often. André slapped his thighs like his great huge brother (whom he so worshipped) Claus. 'La, la,' he went on, laughing. 'Or maybe in America—in America everything is so big.' André went on laughing. 'So you make fun of our poor little mountain *hérisson*. Why, do you have them like a— like a—mountain? A mountain,' continued André, 'does some- times look pricked all over like a *hérisson*. Your mountains in America are, maybe, all called *hérisson*.' Now Madge really was getting a little bored with all this. 'Well, André,' she said, 'I am glad it so excites you. I'm glad you think it funny.' 'What, anyhow,' thought Madge, '*can* be so funny?'

Now Madge was really just a little bit hurt. There is a way of laughing behind cheek-bones that you keep in Leytaux for *fou* English and the *fou* kind of American and the *fou* French. That laughter was shared with other people behind doors and never came out into the open, or if it did come out it gave you due warning, like Belle the cuckoo in Madame Beaupère's clock. Laughter that went on and on like this, laughter that got two or three of the woodcutter's great boys behind a woodpile, was all very well if you just happen to know what it all means. André and Claus very often spluttered jokes, and sometimes, following their funny wood-French, Madge could laugh too, sometimes not understanding half why it should be funny, but all the same being part of the great wave of wild laughter that sometimes shook all the woodcutter's boys like a wind that starts one tree, and then another tree, all blowing. Madge was very near the hearts of Claus, of André, of Fritz, and of very-big Lorenz. All these boys were sort of Pan-boys and

Pan-gods set in a row, like you used to set up statues in Greek temples (it was all in the book Bett had) and before garden gates. Such Pan statues were everywhere in woods in Greek light-in-lamp days, and here on the hills they still walked and laughed and were real people. Bett said, too, that Lorenz was very like a Syracusan goat-boy.

Now all the laughter of all the great Pan-boys was mocking one very white and very angry little wild girl. 'I won't,' said Madge, 'be laughed at.' All the same, she couldn't for the life of her so demean herself as to let André see that she didn't know in the least what was a *hérisson*. 'You, André, and your silly, silly laughter. Some god maybe will change you to a silly laughing bird or a silly laughing jackal for making fun of me, of *me*, Madge.' Still André went on laughing. 'Of course, I know,' said André, 'that you have boa constrictors in your back gardens in—in America——' The very sound of the word America sent André off. 'I know that,' said André, 'therefore it is evident that you must have a *hérisson* the size of a—of a'—and here André choked quite painfully—'of a—a elephant.' Something caught André about the knees and he lay in the grass, screaming. 'You have *hérissons* like elephants in that great country!'

Madge looked at André. Then, with a swift little wild-wood turn and a bird-wing of a swift fling downward, Madge flew rather than ran or climbed right into Doctor Blum's back garden.

DOCTOR BERNE BLUM

14

Now, just as if everything had been going on just the same since the last time, Madge fell rather than climbed or walked into Doctor Blum's back garden. Things were going on just the same as last time, as if there never could have been a time she hadn't been there. The same white boy held the same white fish, the same other white boy held the same other white, dead bird. The two statues of two marble boys stood the same on either rim of the oblong fountain basin, and the same jet of water rose and fell, rose and fell, spraying the flowers about the edges of the basin. Nothing was changed, nothing had ever changed in Doctor Blum's back garden; nothing would ever change, though all things changed swiftly; they changed (in Doctor Blum's back garden) like cloud into cloud, like day into day, so that falling rather than walking into Doctor Blum's back garden you said, 'Why, now, it must be spring' or 'Now it must be summer.' Falling rather than walking, flying rather than climbing from the stream-bed at the top of the high hill, things always looked the same, always looked quite different. Looking into Doctor Blum's garden, winter or spring or summer, you looked for some reason as through mist, softly; slowly the clouds altered, softly, slowly the roses flowered where yesterday there was lilac. Softly, slowly a little girl climbed to her somewhat bashed and mangled little hind feet. Softly, like someone in a dream, she wandered toward the open door and, looking in, wondered what had happened. Had she just now run away from André? Where was André? André would never dare laugh now at Madge who had flown rather than climbed down that last, most intricate, bit of mountain. Slowly wandering and standing peering into a great room, Madge wondered what had happened. Yesterday, to-day? Spring, winter, summer? Growing up and last year's shoes that didn't fit this year—these were things that were part of a dream, not part of reality. Reality was the Erlking and the moonlight on Bett's room wall. Reality was the water that rose and fell, that rose and fell. Reality was the moment that spring turns and waves farewell to summer. Reality was waiting for a moment—for a moment . . . Doctor Blum said, 'Why, dear me, it's Alpen-rose come back with summer's coming.'

Doctor Berne Blum was standing in the wide, cool doorway of Doctor Blum's house that looked such a tiny house from Leytaux up above, that was really quite a huge, big house when you stood in the doorway, not sure why you had come, somewhat dazed with a long walk and a long argument with André and the sun at the back of your head and the cold, cold spring water that had fallen so cold and pure and white that it had looked like a bit of glacier running right through the deep green bushes. Doctor Blum had a teapot in his hand and was watching a little bird that spluttered in the shallow, wide basin where the two white boys were standing. 'Little Alpen-rose,' he said, 'now just how did you get here?' Doctor Blum went on looking at the little speckled yellow and brown bird as he felt for the window ledge with his brown teapot. Doctor Blum put down the brown teapot so quietly that it made no little scrape of sound of teapot on stones, which is such a scraping sound, having tea in the garden, that birds and lizards turn and flinch away. Doctor Blum then went back into the house and reappeared with a flat table with legs fastened under, like mamma's old nurse Rosa used to have for her little sewing table. 'You have a table like nurse Rosa.' 'Oh,' said Doctor Blum from Berne, 'I? And will you help me like I am sure you helped nurse Rosa?' Madge was very pleased to be asked to help, and then she realised that it was day after yesterday, and that it was teatime again like it had been yesterday when all the trouble started. 'You see, it was that hateful Miss Hayes.' 'But such a nice lady,' said Doctor Blum, 'and with *such* pretty hats.' Now, how could this have happened? 'You *know* Miss Hayes?' 'You mean the kind Miss Hayes who works for the English orphans?' 'Oh!' 'Why, yes—she was here but yesterday. She told me she had just then seen your mother.'

Now this was really dreadful. Now what had Miss Hayes told him? 'Just what did Miss Hayes tell you?' Doctor Blum looked very kindly at the little girl. 'She said she had been having tea up at Leytaux with lovely Mrs. Morton and lovely young Mrs. Morton was always so kind about the work and helping, and had given Miss Hayes a lot of pretty things that had grown too small for Alpen-rose, and Miss Hayes said it was so fortunate for the poor Smith-Jones family that little Miss Morton grew so very quickly.' Now, had Miss Hayes really said that? 'Did Miss Hayes really say that?' 'Why yes, why not, Alpen-rose? Now you must stay and have tea.'

RÖSELEIN

15

Now this was really very, very dreadful. Suddenly, sitting outside under the great chestnut tree that was almost over flowering and listening to the fountain splashing and splashing, and looking at two tall, slim Greek marble boys who were only French marble, not Greek boys (Doctor Blum had said), but who reminded Madge of all the pictures and of Pan and Narcissus in the books that Bett had, Madge thought, 'How very, very dreadful.' A little thing that might have been sadness, that might have been hunger, that might have been reproach, that was something of all these

things, ate around her heart, though it couldn't have been hunger,
for little cakes and little cups of tea and more tea made Madge
very cosy and snug where her heart was. Or was it where her
tummy was? Her heart and her tummy were oddly separate. Her
tummy was cosy and comfortable and her feet were cosy and
resting on the grass under the little folding table that she had
helped Doctor Blum unfold and spread so carefully with two little
cups and the little plates and the jar with a big gilt bee on its glass
lid for a handle that she knew held the lovely mountain honey.
Madge was comfortable and uncomfortable at the same time and
at exactly the same place, a place above her tummy, where she
supposed her heart was. It was a sort of lump that came in
swallowing. 'I have been very naughty.' Doctor Berne Blum looked
up and held the tiny bit of bird bread poised in his thin brown
fingers. 'Oh, Alpen-röselein. Surely an Alpen-röselein never could
be naughty.' 'I—*I* have been.' 'Perhaps you forgot for a moment
that you were an Alpen-rose and turned into little Alpen-röselein
prickles. *Bie die Rosen gleich die Dornen stehn*,' and that being
German, little Madge looked up a moment, a little puzzled. '*Bie
die?*' 'By the roses,' repeated Doctor Blum, in his Berne French,
'are still the thorns standing.' 'Oh,' said Madge, 'like *tout épine a
sa rose*.' 'Yes,' said Doctor Berne Blum, 'just exactly like *tout
épine a sa rose*, yet somehow very different.' '*Bie die Rosen gleich
die Dornen stehn*,' Madge repeated and repeated after Doctor
Berne Blum, for the German words sounded rich and deep, and

sounded right coming from the throat of Doctor Blum, just right and beautiful and fitting in with the sun that fell in rich gold spots across the little table. The gold bee and the rich gold spots lying on the table-cloth, and the fall and rise and the rise and fall of the fountain were so a part of 'Alpen-rose is part of everything.' Beauty was, Bett said, different in different things, and the beauty of the German words about the thorn and the rose was deep and rich like the deep gold of the rich spots of sunlight on the little thin table-cloth, and like the great old gold gilt bee that was a deeper gold than the thin beautiful yellow of the honey in the glass jar. 'Everything seems right when I come here, Doctor Berne Blum. Maybe you change people and things and make them right. Maybe you changed Miss Hag Hayes.'

'Miss?' Doctor Blum questioned, arching his black brows under his gray-black shock of wind-blown fine hair. 'Miss *who*, what exactly?' 'I call her,' said Madge defiantly, 'an old hag.' 'I do not, I think, rightly understand that word, my Röselein.' 'Hag. It's a sort of witch. It's a horrible old person who doesn't understand anything,' repeated Madge, piling up the horrors. 'It's a person who comes to tea when she isn't wanted——' 'Surely your sweet mother'—— 'Mamma *said* it was all right, but she was really busy. I saw her face when she put away the music. I was busy too. Why couldn't one just say as the great people do from Lausanne and from Paris and from Geneva, "Not at home", as Madame Yvette's Marie says they do when the wrong people come to see you?' 'Ah, that,' said Doctor Berne Blum, 'is not possible here at Leytaux. Neither at Leytaux on the hill nor Leytaux on the lake. That is not possible,' said Doctor Berne Blum, flicking the last of the bird crumbs to the little wild yellow- and gold-brown little wood bird, 'because shall I tell you, Röselein? We cannot say "Not at home" to the wrong people. For neither at Leytaux up the hill nor Leytaux by the lake are there any wrong people.' Madge knew she had been very naughty and she was going to say so. But she rather wished that she had said so sooner. 'Yes. I do know. But, you see—I mean, I want a hedgehog.'

IN THE MIRROR

16

Now, there sat Madge, again being snubbed, or having been snubbed. The snub was so very gentle, so very, very gentle that it melted away just as swiftly as it came, and Madge in a moment found herself chatting very confidently about a thing she didn't know anything whatever in the world about. The *hérisson*, it appeared, had had baby *hérissons,* rather like a rabbit or a mole or a mouse, so it wasn't anyway (she had found this out) a thing like lavender to put in the linen cupboard or a thing like moth-ball to put in the great chest when one put away one's woollies and Bett's fur coat that was like a soft, very cosy sort of gray-and leaf-brown animal, and that always smelt a tiny bit of moth-ball. The fur of Bett's coat and the idea of the *herisson* having had babies got mixed up in Madge's little confused mind with the memory of André and how silly he had been screaming about mountains and America and England. Was it possible that a *herisson* was a huge thing, though, after all, not as big as a mountain, but maybe as big as the animal that was Bett's fur coat? 'Where—where did you kee-eep them?' Madge asked, for that was one way, and a rather clever little way really, of finding out how big or about how big it might be.

'Oh', said Doctor Berne Blum, 'I had them in the old hawk cage,' and then Madge (whose little mind had mixed up every-thing) remembered the eagle and how it had swirled and swirled, and though it hadn't really been God, certainly it might have been (for André had seen it and so seen her) a sort of messenger of God, sent by God to warn André that a fool *anglaise* little female of an idiot was lost, or about to be lost, on the Leytaux hillside. 'Are *herisson—herissons* messengers like eagles?' 'Like what, Rose-of-the-Alps?' 'Are *herissons*, I mean, mixed up like eagles with stories out of Greek books?' Now Doctor Berne Blum was an odd sort of person. Most people laughed when you asked them questions (even Bett sometimes) or said, 'Little girls shouldn't ask such things' (even Bett, though not as often as most people) or pretended not to have heard, and talked about something else or just went out and whispered (rather loudly) behind doors, 'Now what does one tell a child about such matters?' Doctor Berne Blum wasn't like any of these people. He said: 'Little Rose-of-the-Alps, that is a most important question.' It was interesting to Madge to think that after André's laughter her question was important. '*Hérisson*. I do know your Greeks had ferrets, moles, mice, cats. I don't know yet about a hedgehog.' He repeated 'hedgehog' in his soft, beautiful Berne sort of half-French, and said, 'Shall we go look now before we've quite forgotten?' 'Oh, yes,' said Madge, feeling frightfully important. Doctor Berne Blum went first with the heavy teapot and the clumsy honey jar, and Madge followed with the little teacups and the two plates. A bird perched on the little teacloth, and when Doctor Blum saw it he said: 'We won't shake the cloth yet; we'll leave the table for another minute.' He put the teapot and the honey jar down on the top of the long low wooden chest, and Madge placed the cups and saucers with it. Then Madge followed Doctor Blum sedately.

Doctor Blum led the way down a little corridor that was hung with old coloured prints of birds and bright old-fashioned plates of coloured flowers. There was a humming-bird with wide crest and a tiger-lily half split open to show how the seeds formed in the cup of the flower. There was another bird that looked like a canary swinging on a stalk of wheat, and next to it another flower that looked like a thistle and had a butterfly poised on it. Next the flower that looked like a thistle there was another bird, and so on.

Madge hadn't time to examine each bird and each flower in the half-light of the little twisted passage, but she made up her mind she would when she came out. There was a tiny, very high table at the end of the corridor, and a blue-and-green tall jar that was something called Ming, and had a branch of feather-grass stuck upright in it. The feather-grass reflected feather-grass in a long very narrow mirror placed above the long narrow high table. Out of the long narrow mirror Madge looked at Madge behind a stalk like a little tree of smoke-coloured silver and pearl and gray feather-grass. Madge, looking at Madge, saw Madge go a sudden gold, and across the Madge in the mirror all the little scratches and specks showed in the very old surface of the old narrow glass. Doctor Blum had opened the library door and light poured out and the sun was setting, Madge knew, across the mountains and pouring all its extravagance of gold into the very long high windows that opened out into the balcony of Doctor Blum's long library. Madge followed Doctor Blum, leaving the other Madge shut up in a gray-green surface behind a feathery gray-and-silver plume of swamp grass. 'I feel so funny—leaving that other Madge behind the plume-grass.'

There was never a thing that Madge said that Doctor Blum was not interested in. Now Madge was so used to talking to herself, in English if there were French people about, in French if there were English about, that she hardly every stopped to think if people listened, and, as a matter of fact, people hardly ever did listen to Madge talking to Madge. It was somewhat a surprise to have Doctor Blum turn swiftly: 'What, what was that thing, Alpen-rose?' 'I was saying to myself,' said Madge, 'that I left Madge.' And suddenly it seemed to her that Madge was in so many places. She was here certainly standing on her two little bare feet, facing a window through which streamed the gold-and-amber rare light from the late spring sunset. She was in that mirror and she was still sliding down a dark shadowy passage snatching glimpses of those lovely pictures, a bit of bird, a butterfly, the edge of a sort of morning-glory blue flower. She was here and she was there, for suddenly, it seemed to Madge (she mixed things in her thoughts so) that she was seated on cool grass and a stream was purring and purling and pulsing just beside her. It seemed that her little hand, held up in that gold sunlight, felt the rush of cold cold water, and she thought suddenly again of André. 'I left Madge—and André. I had quite forgotten.'

FINDING A BOOK

17

Now Doctor Blum, finding a book on one of the middle shelves that ran the whole length of the wall opposite the windows, opened the book and looked at Madge over the top of the big book. 'What was it that we wanted?' 'We wanted—we wanted—*hérisson*,' said Madge, still not really knowing what she did want except now it was a little animal that lived like a rabbit, or a big caught bird in the big sort of cage hutch that Doctor Blum had built over against the other side of his garden where the garden stopped against a solid wall of rock that was the Leytaux hill side. Doctor Blum, looking up, looked through and into a little girl standing gilded like that great bee on the honey jar with gilt and amber sunlight. 'Alpen-rose. A *hérisson* was used by the warriors of Mycenæ, who made caps of his rough skin. A *hérisson* was also used in the Athenian markets for the combing of wool; is that what you wanted?' Madge was just a little less wise now than she had been. 'Well, it's a Greek—Greek thing, anyway. And perhaps it was a messenger.' 'A messenger?' Doctor Blum inquired, having, it appeared, forgotten about the eagle. 'Oh, a messenger'—he remembered—'like—like what, exactly, Röselein? 'I mean a sort of thing that—that helps people. I mean, like the eagle was a messenger of God, and the cuckoo was God, and the swan was God too, when he was most white and beautiful and had Helen and Cassandra, who made the war of Troy, and the messengers who are called Oreads, and the messenger——' 'Stop, stop,' said Doctor Blum, pretending to be very much unsettled. 'Really, Alpen-rose, you must tell me all this.' 'Don't you know—don't you know really?' But Doctor Blum did know, Madge saw, by the wrinkles around his eyes and by the way he kept on smiling. 'Oh, you do, you *do* know—everything.'

Now it was very disappointing to Madge to find out for the hundredth, or the hundredth and first, or even the thousandth time, that there was something else that Doctor Blum knew perfectly. 'But you didn't *really* know about the hedgehog?' No, Doctor Blum was very pleased with that. He hadn't really known that the hedgehog was used to comb wool in the Athenian markets and as a sort of helmet for the warriors of Mycenæ. Doctor Blum chuckled very hard, and then was bent a little double, chuckling. 'Röselein, I often wonder who really was your father. You come out with things like one of the fortunate half-children of Olympus.' Now what did Doctor Blum mean by fortunate half-children? 'You mean God and men, or God and women having children—like—like . . .' Then it seemed to Madge quite clear. 'You mean like all of us who have only a Father-which-art-in-Heaven for a father?'

A VOICE

18

Now this very interesting discussion was interrupted by a voice, and it was the very same voice that had interrupted her up the hill side, and that had cut across her rather jumbled, very frightened little prayer which was to Our-Father and Pan and the *Weltgeist*. Just as if the *Weltgeist* and Pan and Our-Father were listening all the time to words, to thoughts, this voice seemed to cut across, to come across just at the very moment when one was hoping for an answer. Madge had half hoped for an answer from *Weltgeist* up the hill side, she altogether hoped for an answer from

Doctor Berne Blum. The same 'who-eee' answered her now as did then. So, of course, it must be André. 'I ran away from André.' The 'who-eee' got louder, seemed to come from the back garden where the little table still stood with its worn thin fine cloth where the little bird had been perched looking for tea crumbs. If the little bird had not flown away long since, while Madge was looking at the morning-glory and the red lily pictures, and the picture of the bird on a thin stalk of something that looked like an ear of wheat, he must have done so now, quite suddenly. For 'who-eee,' rushing into Doctor Berne Blum's quiet back garden, was enough to scare away any bird from tea crumbs or any green and steel or green and gold, or just green lizard sunning on the rocks that were the rock garden the other side of the garden opposite the fountain. Rock flowers grew in the rock garden, Madge knew, all spring, all summer, all autumn, and almost, really all, all winter. André had a way of finding rare and lovely glacial plants and wild wood roots for Doctor Blum, and Doctor Blum knew André and his 'who-eee' almost as well as Madge did. Doctor Blum stopped looking slightly puzzled at what Madge had been saying. Even Doctor Blum sometimes was glad not to have to answer little-girl questions. He looked at the little girl, and then turned toward the wide-flung window. 'That must be our wild-wood spirit,' he said to Madge, standing back in the big room. 'Now don't you think it's André?'

'Oh, it's André all right,' said Madge, 'but I don't want to see

him.' 'Not see wild-brother André?' 'Well, you see, I ran away—
I ran away from André.' 'Why, Röselein, did you run away from
André?' 'Well, you see,' said the little girl, standing back in the
shadows of Doctor Blum's big, cool room, 'he laughed about the—
he laughed about the—hedgehog.' Of course, Madge said hedgehog in her nice French, and Doctor Blum repeated, '*Hérisson*?'
'Yes; you see, he—he'—then Madge didn't know how to continue further—'he seemed to think I didn't know—didn't know
what was—what *was* a hedgehog.'

Now it was all out. Madge ran a little Madge-flight of swift,
little bare footsteps across the room to the window and to the wide
balcony where Doctor Blum was standing. 'Don't, oh, don't tell
him that I *don't* know.' 'Why, my dear little girl,' said Doctor
Blum, seeing that tears were almost about to come to the wide
eyes of Madge standing and staring up at him so tragically,
'why, my dear, *dear* little girl. Now why should that upset you?'
'Oh, I don't know. I do know. It's so mixed up with everything.
With all day.' 'But what a lovely day,' said Doctor Blum, looking
out across his balcony toward the great mountains that rose pure
and blue and silver and cold and rocklike out of the blue lake
that was getting violet-blue where the shadows of the great hills
fell across it. 'I will lift up mine eyes unto the hills,' said Doctor
Berne Blum, 'from whence cometh my help.' He said that in
French, he repeated it in German. 'Those lovely hills,' said Doctor
Berne Blum. 'But come. We'll find the hedgehog.'

PRAYER TO THE MOON

19

André was waiting for them by the outer doorway. He hardly had
time to say, '*Bonjour, Monsieur Docteur,*' politely to Doctor Blum
before he fell on Madge. 'Madd,' he said for the some hundredth
time, 'you are one big fool.' Madge looked at André defiantly,
feeling that even if she didn't know what a *hérisson* was, she now
had Doctor Blum to help her, and anyway, there were lots and
lots of things that André never guessed at, the shapes of sea-shells
and the way the thin-legged sea-birds run along the sand shelf,
for instance, and the sound of a train running into a long, long

tunnel when you come from England, and the different sound the train makes when it runs out of the long tunnel. André was really very stupid, but just because he was so big, and just because he had Claus and Lorenz for brothers and Madge had no brothers (not even any sisters), Madge always felt that André was superior. 'You needn't think—you needn't think . . .' said Madge, and wondered what she had been about to say to André. She had been about to say, 'You needn't think I don't know what *is* a hedgehog,' but she stopped just in time, for she knew that André would guess immediately that she wouldn't take the trouble to say she didn't know if she did know. 'You needn't think,' she said, 'that I stumbled once on the down path. And I got here much, much quicker.' 'I am not going to talk about the down path,' said André, 'but this. You are one big fool, Madd. And your mother now will whip you.' 'My mother never whips me.' 'Well, that is the reason that you are growing up one big fool. You left your boots up there and I left them where you left them.' 'Oh, André, André,' cried the little girl, suddenly remembering all the tiresome trouble those very big-little hobnailed boots had brought her. 'Oh, André; I'll have to go right up there now and get them.'

Madge remembered the thick bushes, the rocks, the trail of the little stream that looked so lovely in the sunlight and in the shade of the thick, green summer bushes, but that, she knew, would be cold and distant and frightening in the evening shadows. All the long, long way back that was such a short, short way down, came to her, all jumbled up with remembered prickles and how dreadfully troublesome those wearying boots had been and the fact that she had been (André was right) one big fool so stupidly to forget them. They must be lying there now by the peacock tail of the white peacock of a little river, and maybe even they had slipped off the lush thick grass into the running water. The thought of boots lying at the bottom of a stream or whirled headlong down the rocks to fall with a horrid dull thud onto the lake side, and maybe be swept out and under the deep lake water, made Madge feel very lonely, very tired, very sick at heart. Evening in Bett's room with tea over and the tea crumbs swept up and the piano making piano-music in the far corner and Madge with a book curled up in the deep divan under the bright light was one thing. Evening creeping up across mountains however beautiful, and miles of prickles to climb over and the heavy rocks to tear one in the half-dark was another. Up above the mountains, so slow, so light, so faint and yet so clear and fair-defined, a globe rose, swam a little as if hesitating, finished its hesitation and swung full on and steadily full up into the silver light that was the just-evening clinging like a veil to the summit of the mountain. Just-evening was silver and into it trailed silver. 'The moon,' said Madge to herself, 'is the goddess Artemis, and the moon', said Madge aloud to Doctor Berne Blum (totally ignoring André), 'loved girls, little girls and big girls, and all girls who were wild and free in the mountains, and all girls who ran races just like boys along the seashore.' Doctor Berne Blum had disappeared, Madge knew, but Doctor Blum had reappeared, Madge felt, for though she faced the lake and the mountains, she felt the little quiver in the air that one feels when people pass near, especially people one loves very much, as Madge loved Bett and as Madge loved Doctor Berne Blum, and even, though in a very different way, as Madge loved her wild-wood friend and wild companion, André. 'The moon,' said Madge again to Doctor Berne Blum, whom she knew was standing there and whom, she knew, knew all about Artemis anyway, and all the little wild things loved of this rare goddess, 'loved all wild things, so she must love me, loved all, all wild animals and little fishes in the sea and lake fishes, and all the wildest great sort of bears and deer, and even wild eagles who plunge down and steal kids and little sheep.' The moon swam up and up, and *Weltgeist* seemed part of the moon and Pan seemed part of the moon, and 'Oh,' said Madge, half to the moon, half to *Weltgeist,* half to André, half to herself, half a sort of little hopeless prayer to anyone, 'why, *why* did I leave those old shoes? Moon, give me back my old shoes.' 'Why,' said Doctor Blum, 'why do you ask the moon to do you favours?' And, whirling on her little bare heels, Madge saw that André was doubled up with laughter, so doubled up that he showed what he had been hiding. 'Oh, André, how can you be so naughty?' For André swung her big-little boots out at her, jeering and laughing: 'Why do you ask the moon for things, foreign idiot, that André himself can get you?' And Doctor Berne Blum was saying: 'Here, Röselein, is your hedgehog.'

André carried the box carefully the long way back, and Madge stopped now and again to hold the box against her face and hear the scratch-scratch of long prickles against the side of the cardboard box. It was the most fascinating sound, and she wanted to carry the box, but André wouldn't let her. When they got back Madge was too tired even to talk to Bett, too tired for anything, too tired even to sit up at the little table under the lamp where Bett made André sit and have brown bread and a bowl of hot soup with her. Madge fell half asleep on the divan, remembering everything, remembering nothing, thinking of André and his 'Now *this* time I tell your mother.' Was it a dream or part of everything, part of the silver mist and the little roses that just were not Alpen-roses, and the boy with a bird and the marble boy with a fish, and the Madge looking out from behind feather grass, and the sound of the hedgehog's porcupine quills made against the pasteboard box, or was it André speaking? 'I would not scold her too much,' was the strange voice of André speaking, 'Madame-the-mother-of-Madd. She is clever on the hill-path. I would not scold her too much, we were late because we—because I got stuck on the hill-path. We were—we were late because we got lost, you see—we got lost, you see—going to find the hedgehog.'